Dear Parents:

The **Ready Reader Storybooks**™ were created especially for children in kindergarten through second grade. This series is designed to increase children's reading skills and promote their interest in reading by themselves. The stories are enjoyable, with easy-to-follow plot structures and familiar settings. Colorful illustrations help develop young imaginations while adding visual appeal to the reading experience. Young children will be comfortable with the format and the large type.

With a variety of stories to accommodate individual interests, the **Ready Reader Storybooks**™ can help develop basic abilities and encourage your children's independent reading.

Tommy Stays Up Late

Written by Eugene Bradley Coco
Illustrated by Robert Sabuda

Modern Publishing
A Division of Unisystems, Inc.
New York, New York 10022

Tommy had a busy day.

He went to school.

He played in the park.

He did his homework,

and he cleaned up his room.

Now it was time to go to sleep.

But Tommy was not tired.

He decided to stay up late
and watch the sun rise.

Tommy took his pillow.

He took his blanket,

and he took his favorite bear.

Tommy even took his flashlight.

Then Tommy put his chair
by the window.

He looked at the sky.

It was very dark.

He looked at the stars.
They were very bright.

He looked at the moon.

It was very big.

Soon Tommy started to get tired.

He rubbed his eyes.

Tommy let out a great big yawn.

"I must stay up," thought Tommy.
"The sun will rise soon."

But Tommy fell asleep.

Suddenly, Tommy heard his
mother calling.

"Wake up, Tommy," she said.

Tommy opened his eyes.

It was morning but it was
still dark outside.

The sun had waited for Tommy.